The Homesick Kitten

The Homesick Kitten

by Holly Webb
Illustrated by Sophy Williams

tiger tales

Remembering my gorgeous Sammy

tiger tales

5 River Road, Suite 128, Wilton, CT 06897
Published in the United States 2023
Originally published in Great Britain 2022
by the Little Tiger Group
Text copyright © 2022 Holly Webb
Illustrations copyright © 2022 Sophy Williams
ISBN-13: 978-1-6643-4042-8
ISBN-10: 1-6643-4042-4
Printed in China
STP/2800/0482/0822
All rights reserved
10 9 8 7 6 5 4 3 2 1

www.tigertalesbooks.com

Contents

Contents

Chapter One
Sammy

Harper sped up as soon as they turned the corner onto their street. She couldn't help it.

"Is he there?" Ava called, scurrying after her, and Harper could hear Mom laughing.

"Yes!" Harper turned to beam at her little sister, and then gave a wave in the direction of their house. She knew it was a little silly to wave at a cat—it wasn't as if Sammy was going to wave back—but it made her so happy to see him there in the window, draped along the back of the couch. "I think he's asleep," she said to Ava. "Oh, no, he's waking up. I can see his golden eyes! Hey, Sammy!"

"Sammy!" Ava bounced up on tiptoe to peer over the fence as the tabby

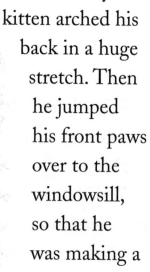

kitten arched his back in a huge stretch. Then he jumped his front paws over to the windowsill, so that he was making a

8

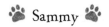

tiny bridge from the couch. The two girls saw his mouth open wide as he meowed excitedly at them, showing little points of white teeth.

Harper didn't think she'd ever grow tired of it. Seeing Sammy waiting for them made her and Ava feel so special. Even if she'd had a difficult day at school, Sammy always cheered Harper up.

When they'd first brought Sammy home from the rescue center as a tiny kitten, he'd had to scramble up the side of the couch like he was climbing a mountain. Mom had watched him do it, and sighed and found a fleece blanket to cover the fabric. The couch was nice and almost new, and she didn't want it covered in little claw marks. Now, a month later, Sammy was big enough to jump to the seat of the couch, and then onto the back, in two huge bounces. It was his favorite place to sit, watching out of the window to see what was happening in the street. Harper figured that he knew everything that was going on.

"Mommy! Come on!" Ava called, and as soon as Sammy saw Mom holding the front door key in her hand, he scooted along the back of the couch and disappeared. Harper felt her mouth curling into a smile. He would be on the other side of the front door now, waiting to wind himself around their ankles, still meowing.

He was wanting his dinner, of course, but it wasn't just that. He wanted Harper and Ava to crouch down next to him so he could climb in and out of their laps and up their school sweaters and nudge their chins with his nose. Once Sammy had even managed to stand on Harper's head, but that was a little painful, because he was too small to understand about not sticking his claws in.

Harper and Ava leaned against the door, giggling, as they heard Sammy meowing on the other side. "He missed us!" Ava said happily, and Harper nodded.

"I'm not sure how such a little cat makes so much noise," Mom said as she turned the key in the door. "Watch out, Sammy!"

Harper peered around the opening

door, checking that Sammy wasn't too
close behind it, but he was so clever
now—he knew about doors. He'd
backed up out of the way, ready to race
to them as soon as they were inside.
Harper kneeled on the floor of the
living room next to him, and Sammy
purred and purred as she petted him.

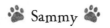

He is so beautiful, Harper thought. She and Ava had fallen in love with him right away when they saw the photo on the rescue center website. Harper had loved the way he looked too small for his huge ears and chunky paws, and Ava thought he was a leopard because of his dark spots. She told everyone in her kindergarten class that they were getting a baby leopard for a pet. One of the boys had come up to Harper on the playground and asked if it were true.

Mom had said she didn't mind which kitten they got, as long as it was friendly. They'd waited to adopt a cat until Ava was at school and a little bit more responsible, but a nervous cat would still find it hard, living with all three of them in a busy apartment, even if they were on the ground floor and had a little yard.

The team at the rescue center had told them that their kitten might be shy at first, but he'd soon relax, and Sammy had. He loved their apartment, and Harper was pretty sure he loved them, too. He was leaning into her hand now, purring so hard that she could feel him shake all over.

"Grandma's coming over for dinner tonight," Mom said as she headed for the kitchen. "So if you have homework for tomorrow, try to get it done now so you can spend some time with her."

Harper nodded and scooped Sammy up with one hand and her backpack with the other. "I've got a math worksheet to do." She followed Mom into the kitchen and said slowly, "Grandma came over for dinner on Monday, too…. Is she okay?"

Mom sat down at the kitchen table with a sigh and looked around for Ava.

"She went to take her uniform off," Harper said. She was starting to feel worried now. Why didn't Mom want Ava to hear what she was going to say?

"Grandma's getting older, Harper, and she misses your grandpa still. She gets tired easily, and going shopping and making meals feels like a lot of effort for her right now." Mom rubbed her eyes, looking tired. "So I've been getting the groceries for her and dropping them off after work, but it's nice for her to eat with us sometimes.

It means she doesn't have to cook, and she gets to see you and me and Ava. It cheers her up."

Harper eyed Mom anxiously. That all made sense, but…. "There's nothing really wrong with Grandma?" she asked. She could hear her voice sounding small and scared.

"No, I don't think so. We just need to take care of her, okay?"

It didn't seem like a very definitive answer, but Harper nodded.

When Grandma arrived later on, Harper kept sneaking glances at her, trying to see if she didn't look well. But Grandma seemed happy to be there, chatting with Ava and making a fuss over Sammy. She did look a little tired, but that was all. Maybe she was having

a good day, Harper thought hopefully,
watching Sammy flop over next to
Grandma on the couch, showing off
his spotted tummy.

"Oh, are you teasing me now?"
Grandma asked him. "Are you going
to jump on my hand if I try to pet that
soft tummy? That's what my old cat,
Bonnie, did, every time."

Harper smiled. "He did that to me this morning." Sammy didn't show any signs of wanting to pounce on Grandma, though. He just collapsed across her skirt, eyes half closed, making wheezy little purring noises as she rubbed his ears and tickled under his chin. "How long ago did you have Bonnie, Grandma?" Harper said, trying to think. "I've seen photos, but I don't remember her."

"Oh, no, you wouldn't." Grandma frowned. "Let me see—Bonnie must have died when you were about two. And before you were even thought of!" she added to Ava, who was curled up at the other end of the couch. "Then for years, I couldn't even think about getting another cat—Bonnie was

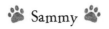 Sammy

twenty, and she'd been with me for so
long. This little love might just change
my mind, though. You're so lucky to
have him."

Harper nodded. Grandma was
right—they *were* lucky. Sammy was
perfect, and he fit into their home so
well. She couldn't imagine any different.

Sammy closed his eyes and slumped
happily, half on, half off Grandma's
lap. He liked Grandma. She was calm
and quiet, and she never decided to
get up and move just when he'd gotten
comfy....

She was rubbing under his chin with
one finger now, just the way he liked

19

it, the same way Harper did. Sammy purred hard, pointing his chin to the ceiling.

Harper was sitting next to Grandma, and Ava was close by, and he could hear Mom humming to herself in the kitchen. Everyone in his family was just where they should be, and he was warm, and full, and sleepy.

Everything was good.

Chapter Two
A Big Change

"Have a nice day, Sammy," Harper said, gently rubbing the top of his head. The little tabby kitten always seemed to want a lot of fuss and attention in the mornings. Harper was sure he understood that they were going to school, and he'd be on his own for a while, so he was making up for it.

"I wish I could take you with me," she told him. "It's Monday, though, which means I have a spelling test. You don't want to come to school today, I promise." Sammy batted at the end of her ponytail and Harper twirled it around for him, laughing as he sat up on his back legs, waving his paws around wildly to catch it. Then he froze as Mom's cell phone started to ring in her pocket.

Mom made a face—she was trying to help Ava get her coat on —but she answered the phone with one hand and held Ava's sleeve out for her with the other. "Hello? Yes…. Oh! Oh, no…."

Harper looked at Mom, and so did Ava, caught by the panic in her voice.

"Yes. I'll be there as soon as I can."

"What is it?" Harper asked, and Ava stared at Mom, her eyes round with worry.

"That was the hospital. Grandma's had a fall." Mom zipped Ava's coat and grabbed her backpack. "It's okay. It's okay. But I need to drop you two off at school and head over there as quickly as I can. I'll have to cancel my shift at the store, but they'll understand…."

"Can't we come with you?" Harper asked, her voice very small. She was thinking of how tired and slow Grandma had seemed over the last few weeks. How Mom had needed to help her up off the couch when she came for dinner a few days before.

Mom patted her cheek. "I know you're worried, love, but I don't think it's a good idea for you two to come to the hospital. We don't know what's happening, and you'd probably just have to sit in a waiting room. They're taking care of her, Harper; she's in the best place."

Harper knew Mom was right—but it didn't make her feel much better.

They dashed out of the house, and for once, Harper was too distracted to blow kisses to Sammy, sitting on the back of the couch, watching them go.

Mom had called Harper and Ava's
school later that morning to let them
know that Grandma was all right—
she'd broken her wrist, and she had
bumps and bruises, but there was
nothing more serious going on. Harper
was still worried, though, and she
dashed out of school at the end of the
day, hoping that Mom would have
more news.

"How's Grandma?" she asked as soon
as she saw Mom on the playground.

Mom smiled at her and waved at
Ava, who was looking around for
them. "Over here, Ava! She's doing
well—actually, I have the car so we can
go and see her."

"At the hospital?" Ava sounded scared.

"Yes, but it's okay, Ava. Grandma's not feeling too badly, and they're hoping she can come home in a few days."

"We can cheer her up," Harper said, putting her arm around her little sister. "I bet it's boring in the hospital."

"Exactly." Mom nodded. "But remember, Ava, we have to be gentle. No bouncing around and disturbing people."

Ava was mouse-quiet for the whole car ride and the long walk through the hospital hallways. Harper had been there once before when she fell off her friend Maya's trampoline, but that was only to the emergency room—the rest of the hospital was enormous, and

Grandma's room seemed to be miles from the parking lot. It was very quiet, and Harper felt like they should be walking on tiptoe as Mom led them over to Grandma's bed.

"You brought them!" Grandma was beaming, and Harper immediately felt better. She'd been expecting Grandma to look really ill, but she seemed fine, except for the cast on her wrist, and she was so happy to see them.

Mom let Ava talk to Grandma for a couple of minutes about the forest school lesson her class had done, and then she broke in—Ava's stories could go on for a while. "Listen, girls. We need to talk to you. Grandma and I have been thinking…."

Harper looked at her worriedly—there was something in Mom's voice, something that meant this was serious.

Grandma smiled at her. "We've had an idea. Don't panic, Harper. Let your mom explain."

"Grandma has a lot of space at her house, and she's feeling a little lonely, now that it's more work for her to go out. And it would be good if there were someone else around, just in case she has another fall. So … we were thinking

28

that maybe we should move in. With Grandma."

"But what about our apartment?" Harper said, frowning. They'd lived in the apartment for so long—she could hardly remember the house they'd had before, when they still lived with their dad as well as their mom.

"Well, it wouldn't be our apartment anymore. Someone else would rent it, and we'd live in Grandma's house."

"You could have your own bedrooms. You wouldn't have to share," Grandma put in, smiling at Harper and Ava.

"My own room!" Ava squeaked. "Can I have purple paint?"

"Maybe." Mom laughed. "Harper? What do you think? I know it's a big change, but you'd love your own room,

wouldn't you? And Grandma's house
is closer to school. Less of a rush in the
mornings."

Harper stared at the blanket on the
hospital bed and tried to imagine living
in Grandma's house, with all of their
things….

"What about Sammy?" she burst out.

Grandma reached out and laid her
good hand over Harper's. "That would
be another wonderful thing for me," she
said. "I'd have you two and your mom,
and I'd have a cat around again. I'm sure
he'll be fine, Harper.
He's only been
with you, what,
five weeks?
He's young
enough to get

used to somewhere new."

"We'd keep him indoors at Grandma's for a few days," Mom added. "Just until he's settled."

Harper nodded, a little doubtfully. Sammy loved their tiny yard. He spent a long time sunbathing and trying to catch bees. He wasn't going to be very happy about staying inside. She realized Mom was right, though. He was going to be really confused when he went out through Bonnie's old catflap and found himself in a whole new yard. It would be better if he got used to Grandma's house first.

"When are we going to move?" Harper asked. She still wasn't sure how she felt about the idea. Even though it made sense, and she definitely wanted to help Mom take care of Grandma, it was such a big change. She needed time to think about it.

Mom and Grandma exchanged a look. "Soon," Mom said gently.

"The doctor we spoke to thinks I need someone to take care of me when I come home from the hospital," Grandma explained.

"But … you said that would just be in a few days!" Harper's voice was a surprised squeak.

Mom nodded. "I'm going to speak to the landlord and explain. We're going to try and move this week."

This week! Harper tried to nod, and smile, but she couldn't imagine living somewhere different in just a few days' time.

 A Big Change

Sammy watched uncertainly as yet
another bag was piled up in the little
hallway of the apartment. He wasn't
sure what was going on. He liked the
bags and boxes—he could jump up and
sit on top of them, and then he was
higher than everyone else, and that was
very good. He was sure there was more
to the boxes than that, though.

Every time he padded into a room,
it seemed to have changed. Furniture
kept moving around, and the apartment
even smelled different, he was sure.
This morning, Mom had whipped his
food bowl away as soon as he'd finished
eating—she hadn't even given him time
to wash his whiskers. The blanket that

33

he liked to lie on along the back of the couch had disappeared, too, and there were no baskets of laundry around to sleep in. Everywhere he looked, something was wrong, and he hated it.

He marched crossly over to Harper, ears flattened and tail whipping, and rubbed the side of his head against her socks. She crouched down to rub his ears, just the way he liked, but she wasn't looking at him—she was still talking to Mom. He didn't like the way her voice sounded—shaky and worried.

"It's going to be so weird. Coming home to Grandma's house after school."

"It's strange for me, too, Harper. I know it's a huge change." Mom sounded different, too, and Sammy edged away a little.

"I'm getting my new room today!"
Ava screeched, jumping from the
bottom step of the stairs and throwing
her arms around Mom's waist.

Sammy darted back, his tail fluffing
up wildly. Harper and Mom were
laughing, but there was an odd feeling
in the air, he was sure of it. Everything
felt jangly and sharp, and it was
frightening him.

He slipped in between two of the

huge boxes, squeezing into the narrow space. It was better, there in the dark. He watched Harper and Ava and Mom set out for school, and he hoped and hoped that everything would be right again when they came back.

Chapter Three
A Strange Place

Sammy had been in his cat basket a few times—that first terrifying journey back from the rescue, which he hardly remembered, and then to the vet for his shots. He hated it every time. He was bigger now than when he'd first traveled in the basket, and braver, so he'd wriggled and squirmed and almost managed to duck under Mom's hands, but she'd gotten the wire door closed just before he managed to dart out of it.

Sammy yowled furiously for most of the ride. He was expecting to be at the vet's again when they got out of the car, but it was somewhere entirely new. He stalked out of the basket, stiff-legged and angry. There was a tiled kitchen floor and piles of boxes everywhere, again!

"Hey, Sammy.... It's okay. Don't worry...."

Sammy glanced up at Mom. Where were they, and why was Mom here, but not Harper or Ava? What was going on? He was so upset that the fur lifted up all along his spine.

"I'm sure you'll get used to it soon,"

Mom said gently, and she petted him, smoothing down the fluffed-up fur and making him feel a little better. He rubbed his chin against her hand and closed his eyes against the strangeness for a moment. She was familiar, at least. Mom fussed around with boxes while Sammy sniffed cautiously at things in the kitchen.

"Here you are, kitten," Mom said, putting his water bowl down next to him. Sammy stared at it. That was his bowl, the bowl he drank from every day at home. What was it doing here?

"Let's give you a little bit of the special food, too," Mom said. "That expensive stuff in the tins that Harper and Ava wanted to get for you. I found it when I was clearing out the kitchen

cupboards...." She rummaged in a box
on the table for a moment and then
put Sammy's food bowl down in front
of him, with something that smelled
strong and delicious. But Sammy
backed away from her. He was hungry,
but he didn't want to eat here. This felt
all wrong....

"Oh, Sammy." Mom looked at him
worriedly. "Harper and Ava will be back
soon. Maybe that'll cheer you up."

Sammy retreated under the kitchen table, where he thought no one could reach him. He sat there all hunched up, glaring at Mom's feet as she hurried around, opening boxes. More things that seemed familiar appeared—there were smells he recognized, smells of home. Why were all these home things here, when this was not home?

When Mom left the kitchen, pulling on the coat she'd left over the back of a chair, Sammy edged out after her, wondering if she was going home. Wasn't she going to take him, too? He meowed worriedly at her, and Mom darted over to give him one last quick pat.

"Back soon, Sammy. I'm going to pick up Grandma from the hospital and then get the girls from school. I have to go, or I'll be late!"

She hurried out, banging the door hard behind her, and Sammy was left alone, staring around him in bewilderment.

Finally he padded back down the hallway, peeking into rooms and sneezing at the dusty furniture. The house felt big, and empty, and wrong....

Harper wasn't sure what to feel when she and Ava got out of school. She was excited and worried and sad all at once.

Her own room! She didn't mind sharing with Ava that much—it was cute sometimes when her little sister wanted to climb into bed with her in the mornings. But she always had to put her breakable things up on a high shelf, just so Ava wouldn't mess around with them. It wasn't that her sister meant to break things, though; she couldn't help it, being little and a bit careless. But now there would be no more Ava deciding to borrow her best pens, just because they were there, and leaving the lids off. No more scribbled-on homework.

It was going to be nice getting to live with Grandma, too, especially now that she needed extra help. They wouldn't have to worry about Grandma being lonely, or maybe having another fall with no one there to take care of her. Grandma was beaming at them from the front seat of the car—she looked so happy that they were all going to be together.

The apartment, though…. It was home. Harper wished the landlord hadn't wanted them to move out on a school day. Even though they'd been able to take things over to Grandma's ever since they'd decided on leaving a few days before, it had still been a rush that morning, trying to wash up and have breakfast in an apartment that was almost all packed up. She didn't feel like she'd had time to say good-bye properly.

At least she'd known what was going on, though. Poor Sammy must have been so confused. She nibbled her bottom lip, listening to Mom explain to Ava that yes, the movers had put her bed in her new room, and her dollhouse, and her pirate costume....

"Is Sammy okay?" Harper broke in when Ava stopped asking questions to breathe. "Does he like it at Grandma's?"

Mom sighed. "I think he's a little upset. He didn't want anything to eat earlier—but we have to give him some time to get used to a new home, Harper. Don't worry. I'm sure he'll be fine."

Harper nodded, but she was still chewing her bottom lip. Mom loved Sammy, Harper knew that she did, but it wasn't the same. Harper was the one

who played with him most, and always
came down in the morning to feed him.
She groomed him and even cleaned
out his litter box. Sammy slept on her
bed most nights now. She couldn't help
feeling that Sammy was mostly hers.
She had to make sure he was okay.

When they pulled up outside the
house, Ava bounced out of the car
and twirled her way to the doorstep,
obviously desperate to run and see her
new room now that it had her things
in it.

Mom unlocked the door and helped
Grandma inside, and they hung up
their jackets on the hooks—they'd
done that so many times before, but
this time it was different. Now this
was their home, too.

Harper had hoped Sammy would come bounding toward her, like he usually did, but no little gray spotted cat raced down the hallway.

"He's behind the basket over there," Grandma said behind her, and then when Harper looked up at her in surprise, she smiled. "I could see you looking around for him. Don't worry, Harper. He'll get used to the new place soon."

Harper nodded, smiling back, and then she crouched down to peer around the basket. A small, angry-looking, striped face glared back at her. Harper really wanted to reach in and pick Sammy up, but she thought she'd better let him come out in his own time. He was grumpy already. He didn't want to be grabbed.

"I could get you something to eat," she whispered to him, her voice soft and persuasive. "Would you like that?"

Mom looked around—she was halfway up the stairs, following Ava. "I put some food down for him before, Harper, one of those little tins. Maybe change it for something else? Maybe he just wants his normal dry food. I'll be down in a minute, Mom. I'll make you a cup of tea."

Harper nodded. And then realized she didn't even know where the bag of cat food was in Grandma's kitchen, and sighed. No wonder Sammy was upset.

"Come on, love." Grandma took her hand. "Let your mom help Ava. She has enough to worry about. I can manage putting the kettle on, and I'm sure there's juice in the fridge. I could pour you some while you see where she's put the cat food. And you can tell me what your day was like. I'd love that."

Harper stood up, glancing back at the basket. Maybe she was getting worked up over nothing. Grandma knew about cats, and she thought Sammy would be fine.

"He'll be here any minute," Grandma reassured her as Harper opened cupboard doors, searching for

the cat food. It was in the cupboard
by the sink, just like it had been at
home—Harper frowned at herself—at
the old apartment, she meant. She had
to start thinking of this house as home
now. They all did.

She pulled the bag out, hearing it
rustle, and looked hopefully toward the
hallway. Yes…. There he was by the
basket—peeking around to see what
was going on. Harper rustled the bag a
little more, on purpose, and then gave
Grandma a big grin of relief as Sammy
came trotting purposefully down the
hall.

Maybe everything *was* going to be
all right….

Chapter Four
A Difficult Time

"Sammy…. Come on…." Harper crouched down by the table and whispered to the kitten. She'd been trying to distract him ever since she got back from school, but it was tricky. Sammy just didn't seem to want to play like he usually did. She picked up one of his favorite toys, a little ball with a jingly bell inside it. Usually if she rolled

it for him, he'd race after it and leap
on it, as if it were some kind of fierce
monster he had to squish. Sometimes
he even tried picking it up in his paws
and ended up doing kitten juggling. He
always made Harper laugh.

"Look, Sammy…. I have your ball,"
she said, holding it up hopefully.
Sammy was sitting by the cat flap,
hunched up with his shoulder bones all
poking out. He glared at her, although
Harper could see he'd definitely
noticed the ball. "Come on," she said
coaxingly, patting the ball against the
kitchen tiles. "Look! I'm going to roll it
for you! Come and see!"

Sammy's tail twitched, and Harper
hid a smile. He *wanted* to chase it, she
was sure.

She'd really hoped that after a week,
Sammy would be settling into their
new home, but it just didn't seem
to be happening. He kept tracking
around the house as though he were
searching for something, and he was
totally confused by the stairs. He spent
a long time sitting next to the bottom
step and staring up, and he hadn't tried
climbing them yet. Harper wanted so
much to pick him up and take him

to see her new bedroom, but she'd resisted. Sammy would get up there eventually, she told herself. It was just that she missed him curling up to sleep in the space behind her knees.

Sammy really didn't like being shut indoors, either. He spent a lot of time sitting by the locked cat flap in the kitchen and banging it with his paw. Then he would look at Harper accusingly. She usually managed to distract him with a toy or a treat, but she was pretty sure that while she was at school, he'd spent a lot of his time scratching the cat flap and trying to get into the yard. Grandma was still feeling tired and a little wobbly after her fall, and she couldn't keep getting up to come and fuss over him.

Harper could understand that Sammy didn't like being shut in the house. She wouldn't want to be indoors all the time, either, but they had to wait until he was settled in. Mom had looked it up and said she thought a week was long enough, so he'd be able to go out in the yard this weekend, when someone could be with him to make sure he didn't dash off and get lost.

At least now it was Friday afternoon, and Harper could spend some more time with him over the weekend.

"Harper, have you finished your unpacking yet?" Mom walked into the kitchen, pushing her hair off her forehead with one hand. She'd been busy all week trying to get everyone settled, and keeping an eye on

Grandma, and going to work. Now she looked hot and exhausted. Harper glanced up guiltily. She hadn't put away much of her stuff at all—just a few clothes. The boxes were still piled up in her room.

"I was trying to cheer Sammy up...."

"I know, love, but those boxes have to go back to the movers, remember? Can you go and start doing it, please?"

"Can't I do it tomorrow?" Harper pleaded. "I'll have a lot of time then. I almost got Sammy to play with his ball a minute ago."

"Except tomorrow you wanted to let him out in the yard," Mom reminded her. "You'll need to be out there keeping an eye on him, won't you? He'll be fine for now, Harper, and it'll definitely cheer him up going outside in the morning."

Harper sighed and headed upstairs. She knew Mom had been unpacking and cleaning and working all day, but she'd been at school, which was work, too. No one seemed to be worried about Sammy like she was. It just wasn't fair.

Sammy padded into the living room, his tail twitching miserably. He'd been about to chase his ball, but then Harper had left again, up the stairs. He didn't like stairs—they felt different, and wrong…. His home didn't have stairs.

Grandma was there, sitting in her favorite chair with a magazine, and she stretched out her hand to him. Sammy bumped his head against her fingers, but he didn't leap up onto her lap. He still felt edgy, and confused, and upset—and even worse, he needed to use his litter box. Back at the apartment, he'd have gone into the storage room and used his litter box, or popped out of the cat flap to the yard, but here it was more difficult. The cat flap didn't work, no matter much he scratched at it, and his litter box kept moving around.

It had been in a corner of the kitchen, and then in a different little room, and now he wasn't sure where it had disappeared to.

He really needed to go. He clawed at the rug, over in the corner of the room away from Grandma. It wasn't the right thing to do, he knew that— but he couldn't help it! What was he supposed to do if they wouldn't let him out? He glanced around guiltily and heard a worried gasp from Grandma.

"Oh, dear, don't do that, Sammy...."

It was too late. Sammy scratched at the rug again and then scooted behind the couch, feeling upset.

"Elizabeth!" Grandma struggled

up from her chair and went out into the hallway, leaving Sammy hiding behind the couch. He could smell the wet patch he'd left on the rug, and it smelled wrong, not like his litter box. He shouldn't have done it.

"What's up? Are you okay?" Mom called down from the landing, and then Sammy heard her hurrying downstairs.

"Yes, yes, I'm fine. Don't panic, love. But Sammy had an accident."

"An accident?" Sammy heard Harper's voice, sounding sharp and worried. "Is he hurt?"

"Not that kind of an accident. He's fine, but he did go to the bathroom on the living-room rug."

"Oh, no…," Mom sighed. "That's just what we need." She came into the

60

living room and crouched down by the rug. Sammy watched her miserably. He could tell that she was upset. "Will this go in the washing machine? I'm so sorry, Mom. Honestly, why on Earth would he do that?"

"It isn't his fault!" Harper marched across the room to stand next to Mom, and Sammy flinched at her cross voice. Had he made her sound like that? "I told you he wasn't happy!"

"That doesn't mean he should go to the bathroom all over the place!" Mom snapped back. "And don't use that rude tone, please."

"But I did tell you!"

"Harper!"

Ava appeared in the doorway and peered in. "Mommy, why are you shouting? What did Harper do?"

"Mind your own business!" Harper growled.

"I think it's my fault," Grandma put in, and Sammy felt his prickly fur settle a bit. Mom and Harper seemed to be caught by her soft voice, too, and they spun around to look at her. "I emptied his litter box," Grandma explained. "I thought I'd freshen it up for him, but then I had trouble opening a new bag of litter with this silly cast on. I was going to ask you or Harper to help me, but it just slipped my mind. I left it on the counter in the utility room. So the poor little love didn't have anywhere to go."

"Oh…," Mom said.

Harper glared up at her. "You see! It wasn't Sammy's fault! I told you it wasn't! I said he was upset!"

"Harper, just go upstairs, please. I don't have the time or the energy to deal with you being rude. Upstairs! Now!"

Harper ran out of the room and Sammy watched her go, his ears flattened miserably. He could hear her stomping up the stairs—his whiskers shook with every thump. Where was she going? Why was everyone so angry?

Mom bundled the rug up carefully and walked to the door, stopping to open the window on the way. "I don't think it went through to the carpet. If we air the room out, it should be okay in a little while. I'll go and put this in the wash and get out his litter box."

"I'll make us some tea," Grandma said, following her out, and Sammy was left alone in the living room, shivering and sad.

Chapter Five
Missing!

Sammy stayed behind the couch, listening to the voices and the footsteps heading off toward the kitchen. He felt utterly miserable. He didn't want to be here. He wanted to be back at the apartment, his real home, where everything was just as it was supposed to be. If he went home, there would be his food bowl and his water bowl and

his litter box, all in the right places,
he was sure. He was so confused and
worried that he thought Harper would
be at home, too—ready to play with
him and let him snuggle up next to her
on the bed. She wouldn't be grumpy
and loud, like she was here.

He had to get back home. Somehow.

The smell of the soiled rug was
still in the room, but there was
another smell, too. A fresh, bright
waft of air, mixed with cars and damp
pavements—an outside smell. If he
could *smell* outside, Sammy thought,
his whiskers twitching excitedly,
then maybe he could *get* outside. He
prowled across the room, following the
smell, and then jumped up onto the
back of the couch to get a better view.

Yes, there! The window was open—
wide open!

   Sammy hardly thought at all, he
simply jumped,
leaping to the
windowsill and
taking a deep
sniff of outside.
He was down
in the flower
bed below
the window
in seconds,
loving the feel of
the crumbly earth under
his paws. He glanced back up at the
window, wondering if anyone had
noticed he was gone, but all was quiet.
Sammy padded across the little front

yard and slipped through the bars of
the metal gate. Out on the pavement,
he paused, sniffing thoughtfully. All he
knew was that he wanted to go home—
he hadn't thought about how he was
going to get there. But some instinct
deep inside him was sure of the way to
go. He knew where home was.

Sammy glanced back at the house
one last time, uncertain for a moment,
but then he scurried away down
the pavement. He could hear cars
rumbling by in the distance—and then
one coming closer, along the street.
He pressed himself back against the
brick wall, feeling the buzz of the
passing car under his paws. He had
been out the front of his old home a
few times, but he'd always preferred

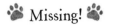

the network of yards and alleys in the back of the apartment. It felt quieter. Safer. He wasn't used to cars, and now his whiskers were tingling with worry. Maybe he should go back—it would be easy to jump up to the windowsill and slip inside. Another car rumbled past....

Sammy shook himself impatiently. It didn't matter. He would stay safely away from the cars. He knew his home was waiting for him, and he was on his way to find it.

Harper lay on her bed with her face buried deep in her pillow. That way she could growl furiously about how unfair

Mom was, and how unfair everything was, and how she wanted to go home, and *probably* no one could hear her. She kicked her feet against the comforter, drumming them up and down—and then rolled over with a sigh.

Mom had put that comforter on her bed the day they moved. She'd chosen Harper's favorite cover, with the unicorn kittens. Her fleece blanket was there, too, folded up by her pillow, because Mom knew Harper liked to hold it while she was going to sleep.

Mom had made sure the blanket was at the top of a box, ready for Harper on that first night at Grandma's house.

Grandma…. Harper sighed again. Grandma really did need them. She'd seemed so happy this week, even though her arm was still painful. She didn't seem as tired, either. She'd loved having Harper and Ava to talk to at breakfast, telling her all about school.

Maybe Harper had been a little unfair, too?

Mom was so worried about Grandma, and she'd had to pack their whole apartment up, and in between doing all that she was on the phone, like changing their address with everyone, and arranging for the movers, and letting the school know what was happening. It was a lot. Sammy going to the bathroom on the rug wasn't actually the end of the world, but maybe it had just felt like it was....

Harper sat up, hugging her knees and wondering if she should go downstairs and say sorry to Mom. Someone needed to feed Sammy, too—he was probably upset about having an accident in the house. Harper went to the door, opening it quietly. She could hear Mom and Grandma chatting in the kitchen, and they didn't sound angry. She would go and give Mom a hug and apologize.

Mom and Grandma both glanced up as Harper came into the kitchen. Grandma was smiling, but Mom looked worried, and Harper's stomach twisted inside her.

"I'm sorry, Harper. I shouldn't have shouted at you," Mom said.

"I came down to say that!" Harper went to put her arms around Mom's shoulders and lean against her. "Are you really upset with Sammy? He didn't mean to…."

"Of course not. It wasn't his fault. I'm just a little tired." Mom sighed. "We should give him his dinner, shouldn't we?"

"I'll do it." Harper got the bag of cat food out and looked around, smiling, expecting to hear a thunder of tiny paws as Sammy came running. But there was nothing. He must still be really upset.

Mom was looking out into the hallway, too, frowning a little. "Do you think he's hiding behind the boxes? He probably didn't like us arguing."

"I'll check." Harper put the food in Sammy's bowl and then went out into the hallway, wondering if he was around the side of that basket again. But there was no sad kitten face peering back at her. Maybe he was still in the living room….

There was no smell, Harper noticed when she went in, so that was good. Then suddenly, something cold seemed to squeeze Harper's insides. The smell was gone because Mom had left the window open. It was still open now, letting in a nice fresh breeze. Harper ran over to it, hoping that somehow it was only just a crack, too narrow for Sammy to wriggle through—but she knew it wasn't.

"Mom!" she yelled in panic. "Mom, the window's open!"

"Yes, I know. I had to let some fresh air in," her mom called back, and then there was a moment of horrified silence, and Mom raced down the hall. "Oh, no…," she muttered. "I didn't even think. Sammy! Sammy!" She looked around frantically.

"He isn't in here." Harper gulped. "I think he went out the window, Mom!"

"It'll be okay." Mom patted Harper's arm, but she didn't sound very sure.

"What's happened?" Grandma came in, and Ava hurried down the stairs to see what was going on.

"Sammy's gone!" Harper turned around from the window. "We left the window open, and we were supposed to be keeping him inside. We have to go and find him!"

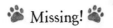

"He's probably just exploring the front yard," Grandma said soothingly.

Harper dashed to open the front door and then ran out into the yard. "Sammy! Sammy!" she called. She was trying to keep her voice calm and friendly, but she could hear it squeaking with panic. They'd been planning to let him out slowly, with someone there watching him and snacks to tempt him back. Now it had all gone wrong. "Sammy, where are you? Mom, can you see him?"

"Not yet," Mom replied. "Let's be quiet for a minute and listen for him…."

They stood frozen on the grass, hoping to hear the jingle of the tiny bell on Sammy's collar, or maybe a confused little meow. But there was no sound at all in the yard—only a car growling by on the street outside the fence.

Chapter Six
Where's Sammy?

Sammy had gone a good distance now, he thought. The kitten could tell he was getting much closer to the apartment, and no one had tried to stop him from making his way there. He would be back home soon, and everything would be right again, he was sure. He would stretch out on the couch by the window and watch the people and the cars passing by, safely far away.

But which way next? Slowly, Sammy twitched his whiskers and then sniffed the air. Yes, he needed to head down here. He trotted briskly along the sidewalk, wondering if Harper would have a bowl of food ready for him when he got to the apartment. He was starting to feel very empty, as if he hadn't eaten for much too long.

The next street shocked him out of thoughts of dinner, though. It was much bigger than any of the small side streets he'd crossed so far—cars were speeding along in a steady stream, with hardly any gaps between them. The wild roaring frightened him, and he couldn't tell how fast they were moving—they seemed to be far away one moment and then screeching past him the next. How was he ever going to get across that?

It seemed a very long way to the far sidewalk, but he was almost certain that home was somewhere on the other side of the street. It felt so close, but he wasn't sure he was brave enough to cross.

Mom and Ava and Harper searched
for Sammy for what felt like hours.
They went up and down the street
calling for him, while Grandma stood
on the patio in the backyard shaking
a packet of Sammy's favorite treats.
They stopped to grab a quick sandwich
for lunch, but Harper just tore hers
into little pieces and nibbled on them.
Her throat felt too dry with worry to
swallow. Sammy was only a kitten—he
was so little! How could he manage
out there on his own, when he didn't
even know where he was?

"He'll probably pop back through the
cat flap any minute, Harper," Grandma
said. Harper knew that Grandma was
trying to be comforting, but it didn't
work. How could Sammy come back

in through Grandma's cat flap when he'd never even been out of it? He didn't know Grandma's yard! *He doesn't even know that this is his home to come back to,* Harper thought, trying to sniff back tears. She wasn't even sure he wanted to come back. He hadn't liked it here—and he hadn't loved them enough to want to stay. That was the worst thing of all.

Mom and Harper went searching for Sammy again after dinner, while Grandma helped Ava get ready for bed. It should have been interesting, getting to walk around the streets close to their new home, and take a look at the playground at the far end of the street, but it was horrible. Especially when every time they passed someone, they had to say they'd lost their kitten, and he was very little, and please could they tell Mrs. Allinson at forty-four Willow Road if they saw him?

"We should make posters," Harper said miserably. "With your number on them, Mom. Then people could just text you if they saw him."

Mom looked uncertain. "Maybe…. I'm hoping that your grandma's right, though, and he'll come home by himself. He could be really close, just a little scared and hiding out. Or he might be shut in someone's garage. Let's give it until tomorrow to start putting posters up. Your grandma has already called all of the neighbors to ask them to watch for him." She sighed. "It's getting dark, Harper. I think we need to get back home."

Harper
slipped her hand
into Mom's.
Both their hands
felt cold, and
Mom looked as
worried and miserable
as she did. If only they
hadn't argued!

*I'd have noticed
the open window if
I hadn't stomped off
upstairs,* Harper thought
miserably, wishing she could go back
and do everything differently. "Do you
think he *will* come back by himself?"
she asked, and Mom hugged her tight.

"I don't know, sweetie. But I'm
hoping. I'm really hoping."

As the night darkened, the passing cars blinded the kitten with the glare of their lights, and they seemed to roar louder than ever. Sammy stayed tucked away under a bush at the edge of the street. The hissing of the tires left him feeling shaky and scared, and he didn't dare face the street. He huddled down in the dust and dry leaves, flinching each time a car passed, until he fell into an uneasy sleep.

He woke up as the sky began to lighten early the next morning and peered cautiously out at the street. He hadn't felt a car rumble by in a while, and everything was very still. The air smelled fresher, and he stretched out his paws, wincing at the stiffness after a night on the cold sidewalk. Home was very close now. If he could drag up the courage to dart across, he would be almost there.

Sammy edged forward to the curb and then out under a parked car. He couldn't hear anything coming.

Go! Now!

He dashed out, racing faster than he ever had before, and flung himself to the sidewalk on the other side. He bounded under a thick hedge, breathing hard but delighted with himself. He'd done it! And now….

He turned his head slowly. *This way? Yes….* He scampered along the sidewalk and around a corner, following that strange instinct inside

him. His huge ears were held high
with excitement. He would be home
soon, and Harper would be there, in
the right place where she should be.
She'd feed him his breakfast; he was
really, really hungry. Then she'd let him
sleep in her lap, or maybe snuggled
between her and Ava on the couch....
There it was! The apartment and his
front window.

Sammy galloped happily down the little path that led to the back of the house and nudged at his cat flap in the back door. It sprang open and he dove through, eager to find Harper and his breakfast.

But it wasn't the same.

He knew it as soon as his paws hit the kitchen tiles—there was a strange smell in the air. Some of the furniture was still there—he remembered when he'd scratched that table leg. But there were new things, too. That big potted plant next to the back door—that hadn't been there before.

It was the smell that was so wrong, though. The apartment didn't smell like Harper and Ava and Mom. It didn't smell like *him*. Sammy edged backward toward the cat flap as he realized. There was another cat here. His apartment wasn't his anymore, he thought, looking around in horror—and then he saw her.

Perched on top of the fridge and glaring down at him. A huge black cat with bright golden eyes. Every hair on her was fluffed out in fury, and Sammy thought she must be at least six times as big as he was. She was hissing now, a long, slow, angry hiss—and then she stretched out her fat black paws down the front of the counter and leaped. Sammy cowered as she landed in front of him, still hissing, and then he turned and hurled himself at his old cat flap, scratching at it in a panic as he heard the black cat yowl behind him.

Sammy shot out into the yard, back arched and all of his fur on end. He could see the other cat watching through the cat flap, but she didn't seem to be chasing him. Not yet, anyway. He scurried back down the path and raced along the street, too scared even to think. At last, he saw a big garbage can on wheels in an alley next to a store and ducked underneath it to catch his breath. What was he going to do now?

Chapter Seven
Looking for Sammy

Harper woke up that morning with an odd sense that something was wrong. It took her a moment to remember what it was, especially as her new room still felt strange. She reached down to pet Sammy—and discovered that the warm lump next to her wasn't Sammy. It was Ava.

Then she remembered everything.

Ava was there because Harper had woken up in the middle of the night to find her little sister crying and pulling on the sleeve of her pajamas. Harper hadn't been able to figure out what Ava was saying for a moment—she was too muffled up with tears—but then she'd realized that it was, "I want Sammy back!" She'd let Ava climb into bed with her and held her until she cried herself to sleep.

"Hey…." Mom had pushed the door open and was smiling at her. "I couldn't find Ava, and I guessed she'd be in here. I'm sorry, Harper; I didn't hear her wake up."

"It's okay." Harper looked up at Mom hopefully. "Is Sammy back? Did you check his blanket?" Grandma had suggested last night that they put Sammy's favorite blanket out on the doorstep so he had something familiar to smell if he were trying to make his way back to the house. Harper had gone to sleep thinking about waking up the next morning and seeing Sammy curled up there, waiting for them to find him.

Mom sighed. "No. I'm sorry, sweetheart. Not yet. I did look."

Harper wriggled out of bed, trying not to wake Ava. "Should we make posters?"

Mom nodded. "Okay. You start making some. I'll get breakfast ready."

"Elizabeth? Harper?"

That was Grandma calling from her room. Harper glanced up at Mom in surprise. Both of them went to look around Grandma's door. "Are you okay, Grandma? Did you want something?"

Grandma was sitting up in bed with a book in her hand. "I'm fine; don't worry. But I had a thought. Before you put up posters, you should go and check the apartment. Maybe Sammy went there. I've heard stories about cats being able to find their way back miles and miles, and it's only ten minutes away, isn't it?"

Harper's eyes widened. "Yes!" she yelped, and then remembered Ava sleeping and put her hand over her mouth, whispering through her fingers. "Oh, yes! Grandma, that has to be right! Can we go now, Mom?"

Mom shook her head. "Not yet. It's too early, especially since it's Saturday. We'll have to wait a little while. But that's a great idea, Mom."

Harper nodded, though the thought of waiting was horrible. "I'll make the posters, just in case. But I bet he'll be there, and we won't need them after all! When we come back with him, I can tear them up into tiny little pieces." She could see herself doing it—or crumbling them up into a big paper ball for Sammy to chase.

Harper had made six posters by the time Mom said they could go, with beautiful cats drawn on them, and a description of Sammy, and Mom's phone number at the bottom. She kept looking between the kitchen clock and the front door, desperate to head back to the apartment. At last Mom nodded at her, and Harper flew to grab her jacket and her sneakers. Ava was still asleep upstairs, but Grandma said she'd listen for her.

Harper wanted to run all the way back to the apartment—she kept darting ahead and having to circle back to Mom. Every time she wanted to say, *He will be there, won't he?*

Mom had brought the cat carrier with her, so she must think they were going to find him. But it was hard to imagine Sammy working his way back through the neighborhoods, especially crossing the main street. Harper wouldn't want to cross it on her own, so how could Sammy do it? There were parked cars all the way up and down the sidewalks, and it was so hard to see. They had to edge out between two cars, and look, and then hurry across.

Harper slowed down again after

that, now that they were really close, and they were about to know. Suddenly, she was scared.

"Come on," Mom said, squeezing her hand. "It's going to be okay, Harper. Even if they haven't seen Sammy, we'll go back and put your posters up. We'll find him."

Harper nodded, but she was holding her breath as Mom rang their old doorbell. It seemed like forever before anyone came to the door, and then a tall man stood there, smiling at them politely.

"Hi!" Mom said, her voice rather high and worried. "I wondered if you'd seen our kitten. We moved out last week— this was our apartment—and he's disappeared. We thought maybe he'd come back...."

"Oh, no, I'm sorry." The man
shook his head, and Harper felt
tears suddenly burn at the backs of
her eyes. "What does he look like?
We'll keep an eye out for him.
Would you like to give me your
phone number?"

Harper stood pressed tightly against
Mom's side, watching a beautiful

black cat stalk out of the kitchen
toward them. She was huge, and
her fur was all fluffed up. Maybe
she didn't like strangers, Harper
thought. Or she didn't like the
apartment, like Sammy didn't like
Grandma's house.

Harper looked back as they walked
away and saw that the black cat was on
the back of the couch, watching them
from the window, just like Sammy
used to.

It made her want to cry, and she had
to hold her hand over her mouth. The
black cat was in Sammy's place, and
her little spotted kitten was out there
somewhere all on his own.

Sammy peered out at the sidewalk and the feet passing by. What was he going to do now? He had been desperate to find home, and now home wasn't there. He'd expected that everything would be the same, the way it should be. Now he knew that it wasn't. The apartment belonged to another cat instead. He shivered at the thought of her angry hiss. Did that mean he didn't have a home anymore?

Sammy huddled himself smaller and tighter. Was he really all on his own? Or maybe—had he been looking for the wrong thing?

It was Harper and Mom who put the food in his bowl. Ava who climbed up on the couch to look out of the window with him. Harper who curled herself around him in the middle of the night and made him feel safe and loved.

He had to find them. His home was where they were; it wasn't a place at all.

But how? He hadn't gotten to know the new house. Did he even know how to get back?

Sammy wriggled slowly out from under the garbage can on the wooden pallet and set off along the sidewalk, trying to remember the way he'd come. He'd followed this wall just before he came to the apartment, he was sure. But then—his ears flattened. At the end of the wall was that big street again and a car speeding by, the tires screeching loudly on the pavement.

Sammy stepped slowly out between two parked cars and stood there, listening. Was it safe to run? The street seemed quiet. He scurried out and then froze in panic for a moment as he saw a car bearing down on him. Sammy flung himself forward, darting to safety just in time. The car sped on—had they even noticed what had almost happened?

He scrambled up onto a wall, shivering at the memory of the car's hot breath ruffling his fur. He licked a paw and swiped it around his ears and whiskers, over and over again, trying to wash away the panic, until at last he felt a little calmer. Then he jumped down and set off again, slowly retracing his steps as well as he could.

It was as he turned a corner that he noticed a faint, familiar scent in the air. Something that smelled like home… Harper. He hurried on eagerly, hoping to see her any minute, but the street stretched on ahead of him, empty and strange.

Had he gone the wrong way? But … there was still that scent.

He was so busy trying to catch it

again that he didn't notice the dog
until they were practically nose to
nose—and the dog seemed just as
surprised as he was. It jumped
back, eyes wide and
ears pricked, and
whined. Then it
crouched down,
stretching out
its front
paws, and
barked
sharply
at him.
Sammy
retreated,
terrified. He'd
never been so close to a
dog, and he didn't know what to do.

The elderly woman holding the leash pulled the dog back. "What's that, Petey? No, leave it alone!"

Sammy hissed faintly and turned tail, racing away through a clump of bushes nearby. He wasn't going to give that huge dog the chance to get any closer.

At last, he looked out onto an open stretch of grass that was dotted with people. On the other side of the grass, swings were moving through the air, and children were calling. Sammy was sure he'd never seen it before. He retreated under the bushes, feeling so tired. He had no idea where to go next.

"But where is he?" Ava demanded, staring at Mom and Harper over her bowl of cereal. She'd woken up while Harper and Mom were back at the apartment and Grandma had told her where they'd gone. Now she just couldn't seem to understand why they didn't have Sammy in the carrier.

"We don't know at the moment," Mom tried to explain. "We'll keep on looking, though. Harper made posters. We'll go and put them on all the lampposts soon. If anyone sees Sammy, they'll know to call us."

Ava only shook her head. "We have to find him. He'll be hungry. He's missed dinner last night *and* breakfast today."

Harper pushed her cereal around her

bowl, blinking back tears.

Ava was right, of course. She was too little to know that it didn't help to say it.

"I've finished my cereal," she told Ava. "Let's go and put the posters up now."

"Give me half an hour, Harper, okay?" Mom said. "I've got the numbers for all of the local vets and the animal rescue center. We should call them first to see if anyone has found Sammy and taken him in."

Harper nodded. That made sense.

"I'll make some more posters then. Or can I go and start putting them up?"

"And me!" Ava jumped up from the table.

"No, not on your own. I'll be as quick as I can, I promise. I know it's hard to wait, but it's important to call the vets. Someone might have found Sammy already."

"I'm going to make posters, too," Ava said, grabbing a piece of paper and starting to draw a kitten, but Harper followed Mom into the living room.

"Mom, can't I just go down the sidewalk and put some of the posters up? It's not far, and I won't cross the street."

Mom sighed, looking at her phone and the list of numbers she'd written.

"Okay. But only as far as the end of the street, all right? Don't go past the park."

"I promise." Harper nodded. She knew Mom was right, and someone might have found Sammy already, but she just couldn't stand to wait any longer. She kept thinking of her kitten out there, lost and confused, and it made her stomach twist up inside her.

Chapter Eight
Home Again

Harper stopped at the entrance to the park, wondering if she should stick a poster up on the fence. A lot of people would see it there, but she wasn't sure how well the tape would work. She held the poster up against the wooden slats, frowning. Maybe there was a bulletin board or something like that at one of the other gates.

"Are you all right, dear?"

Harper turned to see that an elderly couple with a dog had paused on their way out of the park. She nodded shyly. "I was going to put up a poster," she explained. "Our cat is missing. He's a kitten really, a gray tabby kitten."

"Oh!" The woman glanced out toward the street. "Silver? With spots?"

"Yes!" Harper almost dropped the posters. "Yes, he's spotted! Have you seen him?"

The couple nodded to each other. "We did see a little cat. Petey scared him, I'm afraid," the man told Harper. "He's friendly, but the cat didn't know that, of course. We were back up the street that way and then the cat ran off, into one of the yards, I think." He pointed up the street toward Grandma's house.

"That was about fifteen, twenty minutes ago," the woman put in. "I'm sorry that we didn't see exactly where he went."

"But you saw him!" Harper smiled shakily. "Thank you! I'll keep looking."

"Good luck finding him!" the man

called back, waving to her as they set off down the street.

Harper leaned against the fence for a moment. Sammy was okay! They'd seen him—a spotted silver kitten. It had to be him, didn't it? She hurried back along the street, calling hopefully. "Sammy! Sammy, here, boy! Where are you?" She was sure that she'd see him darting out of a yard toward her any minute, but she kept on calling and calling, and nothing happened.

He could have gone farther up the street, Harper decided, especially if it had been a while. She ran along the sidewalk, stopping to peer over fences and under cars, always calling.

About halfway between the park and their house, she saw something gray dart underneath a gate, and she gasped excitedly, running to lean over and look into the yard. "Sammy! I'm here, Sammy, come on!"

Everything was quiet for a few moments, and then a little face looked back at her from behind a tall fern.

It wasn't Sammy. The cat looked like him, but it had a white chin and paws, and it was mostly striped, with a few spots along its sides. It just wasn't her kitten. Harper swallowed hard, gulping back her disappointment. She'd have to keep looking.

She was turning away from the yard when she realized something awful. The elderly couple must have gotten it wrong. They must have seen *this* cat. Young and thin and silver

tabby—it all matched.

No one had seen Sammy after all.

Under the bushes at the edge of the park, Sammy startled awake. He'd heard a voice he recognized. That was Harper, he was almost sure. She was here! She was calling him! He leaped up, racing to the edge of the path, and then checked, looking around for the dog. He remembered its bright eyes and the

118

way it had snuffled after him so eagerly.
Sammy's tail fluffed up to double size
again. What if it was still there, waiting
for him? He was safe here underneath the
bushes—out there he'd be in the open,
with nowhere to hide. He crouched under
the low branches, hesitating.

But he had to follow Harper's voice.
He couldn't miss his chance to go home
again!

Sammy darted out onto the path and
through the park gates to the street,
hoping to see Harper looking for him.
But no one was there.

Harper rubbed her eyes on her sleeve.
She knew crying wasn't going to do any

good, but she couldn't help it—she'd been so excited, so sure that she was about to get Sammy back. That extra little bit of hope from the elderly couple had been torn away, leaving her feeling more heartbroken than ever.

She would go back and see how Mom was doing with the phone calls, she thought sadly. Maybe there'd been some good news. Then she looked down at the poster in her hand and sighed. It had actually been a smart idea to put one up at the park—so many people went through those gates. She just needed to find a better spot than the fence, that's all. She'd do that now, rather than wasting the poster.

"I can't give up," Harper muttered to herself. "We're going to find him. We have to." But she wasn't calling for him as she trudged back down the street toward the park. She wasn't hoping, the way she had been before. She walked on with her head down, just concentrating on not crying.

She was unrolling the poster, ready to tape it to the garbage can by the gates, when she heard meowing—high, frantic, excited meowing. She dropped the poster and the sticky tape, without even noticing that she'd done it. She looked around wildly, her breath caught in her throat—and a tiny, silver spotted cat came racing out from under the bushes by the park gates.

"Sammy!" Harper scooped him up into her arms. "They *did* see you! I thought—oh, it doesn't matter! Where

did you go? We have to get back
and tell Mom. She's calling everyone
about you. Oh, I dropped the poster!"
She scrambled around to pick it up,
while Sammy tried to climb inside
her jacket and nuzzle her, purring and
purring. Then she shoved the poster
into the garbage can and whispered
into the top of his furry head, "Let's
go home."

The house still seemed a little strange—
but Sammy was starting to feel as if he
belonged. His litter box was in a nice
quiet corner now, and his toys were
scattered everywhere. A blanket that
smelled like Harper was draped over
the back of the couch. He could stretch
out on it and see the street, and watch
the birds in the yard, too.

When Harper had carried Sammy
into the house, such a wave of happiness
and relief had swept over him. He could
feel them all loving him—Harper, Ava,
Mom, and Grandma. He'd followed
them around all day, even curling up in
Grandma's lap under the table while
they were eating lunch.

That night, as Ava and Harper had started up the stairs, Sammy had put one paw on the bottom step and meowed.

"He wants to go with you!" Mom had said to Harper, laughing.

"You'd better help the poor kitten out," Grandma agreed, and Harper had scooped him into her arms again and carried him up to bed with her. He'd investigated the bathroom while the girls were brushing their teeth and then followed them back into Harper's room. He liked this room—there was a windowsill, and he thought it might be sunny to sit on tomorrow. So many different places to explore up here. So many interesting smells.

Now he yawned and stood up, turning around a couple of times and padding at the comforter to get it just right.

"Is he okay?" Ava sat up in bed to look at him worriedly, and Sammy nudged his nose against her cheek.

"I think so." Harper smiled at her. "He does that, Ava; it's all right. He's getting comfy. Go to sleep. Mom said you could only come in here with me if you promised not to keep chatting."

Ava lay back down, and Sammy tucked himself into the nest of comforter between both sisters and started to purr. Some things were different, but this hadn't changed. This was where he was meant to be, curled up with Harper and Ava.

HOLLY WEBB

Holly Webb started out as a children's book editor, and wrote her first series for the publisher she worked for. She has been writing ever since, with more than 100 books to her name. Holly lives in England with her husband, three children, and several cats who are always nosing around when she is trying to type on her laptop.

For more information about Holly Webb visit:

www.holly-webb.com
www.tigertalesbooks.com